# BEDTIME FANTASIES II

By Ajaydeep M

No part of this fiction may be reproduced or used in any manner without the written permission of the copyright owner except for the use of quotation in a book review.

# JANE'S FANTASY

It was the year 1985. Jane lived in a beautiful neighborhood with her loving husband Alan. She worked in a quaint bookstore that was just down the block from her house. Generally, she was happy, and her husband also doted on her all the time. But she had a secret that no one knew, maybe not even her.

Jane loved her husband and everything about him. But she always thought that something was amiss. It had been five years since they had been married, but they did not have children, but that was okay. Both of them felt that they had married young and that they did not have to rush into anything. However something was missing, she felt.

Their sex life was not bad perse, it was adequate at best. Not that Alan was not amazing, he really was, but she never felt like she was in a state of an abyss, or that everything had become just a blur after being with him. She never focused so much on it, and just assumed that that is how it is for women. She did not know what to compare it to, as her husband was the only person she had ever been within her entire life.

One day when she was working in the store two girls had come to the store to buy a book. They were rather giggly and flushed when they entered the bookshop. They gave Jane a fleeting image of a newlywed couple that was enjoying their honeymoon phase. But she brushed it off quickly as she thought it was stupid to think like that for a couple of women. It did not escape her mind that they were standing far too close to each other. Maybe they were just best friends she thought and greeted them.

She asked them how she could help them, but they thanked her politely and told her that they were fine on their own. Jane did not mind. She went about reading the book that she was reading before they came in. She tried not to listen to them, but their voices were quite high pitched and even their whispers were very clear.

"Is this the book?" , "I think so." "turn to page 289, that is where it is written Susan said." "Yes, this is the one." These were the snippets she could hear from their conversation. Jane tried her best, but she was curious. What was on page 289? And why were they blushing so much about it? Her train of thoughts was broken when they came to the counter and told her that they wanted to purchase a book.

Jane looked at the book and tried not to give a reaction. It was erotica, which made her even more curious about what possibly be special about one page. Once the ladies were gone from the bookstore, she tried to get back to her book. But, she simply could not focus.

Curiosity got the best of her and she went to the area where they had been standing to see if there was another copy of it somewhere. Sure there was

She took the book and went to her seat near the counter. She closed the blinds next to her seat so that the passersby would not see what she was reading. Her desk was tall enough to hide what she was doing so she did not have to worry about people entering the store when she was reading it.

She directly went to page 289. And she started reading. Her jaw dropped when she  read the first line. It said that there was a woman who was seduced by a lady in her neighborhood. She quickly shut the book close. She was feeling a rush of emotions. Just reading the first line had made her cheeks go red and she was breathing rapidly. What she was not expecting was the tingling sensation in her head. Her ears were ringing and she was contemplating whether she should read ahead or not, but just then a customer entered the store. She decided that she will buy the book and read it at home.

She bought the name under a false name, and carefully covered it in brown paper and put it in her bag, and went home. She was preparing dinner, but her mind was traveling to the book again and again. She was idly stirring a pot when she heard the front door open. "Honey! I am home!" said Alan, closing the front door behind him.

She went to greet him and he gave her a soft kiss on the lips before he went to freshen up. They were soon having a peaceful dinner where they talked about what they did that day. Jane left out the part about the women entering the store, and the book. She never felt like hiding anything from her husband, but she felt like this time it was something very intimate that she did not want to share with anyone yet.

After dinner when Jane was wiping the washed dishes, Alan came from behind and hugged her. "Let's go to bed." He said while nibbling her ear. Jane knew what that meant. She smiled and turned around to kiss him. "Whatever you say," she said. They went into the bedroom. He took her clothes off while she was unbuttoning his shirt. He started kissing her intensely on her lips. He then threw her on the bed and removed his pants.

His cock was erect. He held both her hands and then inserted his shaft inside her. She let out a small gasp. And then he started thrusting himself inside her furiously. Jane liked it, but she did not want it to be so sudden. She wanted him to play around a little bit, she did not tell him that. It scratched an itch for her but it did not make her weak in the knees, or make her limp after she had her orgasm. Meanwhile, Alan was grunting and saying her name again and again.

Jane did not want him to feel bad so she too closed her eyes so as to show him that she was also enjoying it. But, when she closed her eyes the image of the women in the bookstore cropped into her mind. The way they were holding each other's hands.  The way they were standing too close to each other. She did not even realize when she started biting her lower lip. She quickly opened her eyes to get back to reality.

Alan was still pounding inside her and she noticed from the volume of his grunts that he was close. He thrust for one last time and came. He plopped himself near her and asked her, "Was it good for you?" he asked her. "Of course sweety." Jane lied, with a pasted smile on her face. But, in reality, the image of those two women had pierced her more than anything that had happened that night.

Alan instantly went to sleep. But, Jane was awake. The second she tried to close her eyes; she saw those women and the one line from the book that she had read. It was giving her a sensation 'down there.' Something she had never felt after she had been with Alan. She looked over to her side and saw that Alan was fast asleep. She slowly covered her naked body in a sheet, closed the door of the bedroom, and crept over to the living room. Her bag was lying on the table. She opened it and removed the brown package carefully.

She glanced around to the bedroom door and saw that it was still closed. She opened the package without making any noise. She sat on the couch and adjusted the sheet so that it was properly covering her. She sat over there, opened page 289. She started reading it past the one line she was able to read in the bookstore.

The more she read, the more her loins started aching. With every line she was reading, she was getting more and more aroused. Her breathing was ragged. She was biting her lip without even knowing that she was doing it. One hand was holding the book, while the other was caressing her breasts. That book was making her go wild. She had never felt like this before. She never thought that reading about two women having sex with each other would make her wet down there or that it would make her touch her down there.

When she started rubbing her pussy, the sheet
that was clinging barely clinging on her, slid
down. It made her come back to her senses.
She quickly closed the book put it back in her
bag, and went to the bedroom to sleep near
Alan. She tried to sleep but she never felt so
awake before.

When the morning arrived, Jane who hadn't
slept a wink quickly got up, made breakfast
for the both of them. It was a Saturday that
day and she did not work in the store on
Saturdays and Sundays. Lanie picked those
shifts. But Alan worked on alternate
Saturdays and today he was going to go to
work. She bade him goodbye. Quickly had her
breakfast and went for a wash.

She put on her bathrobe.  And made sure that
Alan had locked the door on his way out.
Next, she removed the book from her bag and
took it to the bedroom with her. She sat cross-
legged on the bed and opened it to the page
where she had stopped reading. And so she
continued reading about how a woman was
seduced out of her senses by the lady who
lived across from her house.

Jane had never thought she would be so
aroused by reading something like this about
women. When she was reading about how the
woman was being pleasured, she started
touching her pussy.  She played with her clit.

She was doing it slowly in the beginning and just as the woman in the book started moaning, she increased the speed with which she was rubbing her labia. And soon enough, she was nearing climax.

She let out small gasps when she was nearing her orgasm. And then her entire body shivered and she came. She closed her eyes. For the first time she felt like she was satisfied in a long time. She lay still for quite a while. Then she started thinking, sprawled on the bed about what had happened just now. She had just been driven to an orgasm when she was reading about two women who were doing it with each other. What was more, when Jane was thinking about the woman who was being seduced, she was imagining herself in her place.

She wanted to be the woman in the book who was being fucked by the lady. The mere thought of it was so kinky, but she could not stop herself from thinking about it. She started touching her vagina gain. This time, she was more sensitive than before. She was rubbing her clit furiously with one hand. Her other hand was occupied with pinching her left nipple.

And then she came for the second time in a matter of minutes. She did not remember when she had felt like this in the past ten years. One thing was clear to her then. She like women more than she liked men.

Once she knew her own secret, it felt like everything made much more sense in her life. She loved her husband, but now that she started thinking about it, she had never felt like this about any man, not even her own husband maybe. Now that she knew what it felt like to yearn for somebody sexually, she came to know that she had never thought about her husband like that.

In the coming days whenever she got the chance she would read that book. Not just that book, she had bought similar books from the store. She was a quick reader and she was going through these books pretty fast. Moreover, whenever she was having sex with her husband, she would close her eyes and think about the time she was with herself and she was reading about these women. Now, when she came it was for real, and not because she wanted to show her husband that she loved him.

Jane was very careful to not let Alan see these books. She would hide them on a shelf in the closet. She thought no one would ever come to know about her dirty secret. And she was sure as hell not going to tell her husband. What she and Alan had was special, and she did not want to ruin it.

But, fate had other plans. One day when she was at the bookstore, Alan had come home as he had forgotten an important file at home. He came home and he started searching for it literally everywhere. He completed the search in the living room and moved to the bedroom. He looked on the bed below the bed, near the table, in his cupboard, everywhere. Then he remembered that once Jane had accidentally kept one of his files in her closet with her clothes.

So, he stepped into the closet and started looking around that is when he saw that a shelf was locked. Having searched the entire closet he thought that he would open it and check. He knew that Jane always kept keys nearby. So he reached for it under the carpet in the closet. It was there. He opened it up only to see that it wasn't his files, but his wife's books. Before he could feel the shock of it all, he got a call from his company. He picked the phone. It was his secretary telling him that they had found it in his office itself.

He told his secretary that h won't be coming in, he has some emergency work at home, and that she should give the file to his associate so that he could present at the meeting. His secretary asked him if he was okay, and he said yes. She asked him if there was anything she could do for him. He had not missed her sneaky double meaning in it. He always knew that she had a thing for him. But, he never showed it as he was not interested in her. Not that she was not attractive. She was a pretty blonde who wore clothes that were always a size smaller than her and when she walked around in those high heels her entire body would bounce along with her. But, he did not give her a second thought as his lovely wife was sexy too.

Jane was 5'5" with dark brown hair that went up to her hips. She had a voluptuous bosom and an ass that matched perfectly with it. So, he did not have to look at any other woman ever. She was enough to take his breath away.

But right now, he was in disbelief. He could not understand what he was seeing. He saw that all these books were about women having sex with each other. He did not understand why Jane was reading it, unless…

The thought was like a kick in the gut for him. He realized that his loving wife liked women more. He was very fond of her and he wanted her to be happy. He wanted her to be satisfied in life. And so he decided that he was going to make her dream come true for her. He kept her books back and locked the shelf, and put the key under the carpet where he had found it.

He went back to his office. There were some papers that were going to require his urgent signatures. On his way, he kept thinking about how he could make his wife happy. Once he was in his office, his secretary came in. today she was wearing a salmon shirt which was very transparent, he could see that she was wearing a lacy black bra underneath it which was trying to support her heavy tits. It also did not escape him that she had popped a button on the shirt so that when she bent down she was putting up quite a show. She was wearing an equally tight grey pencil skirt which perfectly showed her outline.

He had an idea. He asked her, "hey Mindy. I had a question for you. It was a little personal." "Sure, you can ask me anything." She said with a come-hither look that was glaringly visible. "Do you have any girlfriends, who like to enjoy among themselves?" He asked, not sure if she would understand what he was saying. But, judging by the tone of her answer, he knew that she had understood. "Yeah, I do. A couple of them. why?" She asked. "I can't tell you that. But could you please give me their number?" he said, not wanting to discuss this with his flirtatious secretary. She gave him the numbers.

He called them immediately and asked them for a favor. They agreed at once. He decided that he would go away for the weekend so that his wife could enjoy the festivities on her own. He deiced to tell her that he was going to go on a business trip. At that time, Mind y came in asking him if she could go home. He was about to say yes. But, he asked her something instead. "sure. I have to go on a business trip this weekend. Will you come with me?" She definitely understood why he was asking that, but she wanted to make sure. "But, I did not know about this before. Is there any work that I would need to do before?" She asked. "Yes. Here is my credit card. By the sluttiest lingerie that you can. And yes, bring two sets. One for you, and well, one for my wife." He said smiling coyly.

He decided that when his wife was going to be out and about, he also should get the opportunity to be with other women. When Mindy bought a set of lingerie for his wife. She came in and to his surprise, sat on his lap. "This is for your wife." She said while slightly brushing his cock with her hand, which instantly started rising by her touch. She leaned in to kiss him. Alan motioned forwards hungrily too. But she just laughed and walked out of the office. Now, he was eagerly waiting for the weekend.

On Saturday, before leaving in the morning, he gave Jane the bag of lingerie and said, "Hey sweetheart this is for you. I want you to use it tonight." She looked confused. "Honey, I know your secret. And it is alright. You do not have to change for me. We will have these weekends more often where you get to do whatever you want, and I get to do whatever I want, rather whoever I want." He smiled mischievously. She kissed him passionately and said, "Thank You. I love you" "I love you too." He said. And saying so he left for his business trip' with his secretary. He knew he was in for an adventure.

Jane looked through the bag. She was shocked to see the lingerie inside. She chose a wine-colored one to wear. It complimented her hair as well as the hazel-colored eyes. She spent the entire day in trepidation. She did not know what to expect that night. So she drew a long bubble bath, cleaned the house, especially the bedroom. And then finally sat wore the wine-colored satin lingerie that she had liked.

She was just about to go into the kitchen to see if there was some wine at home when the doorbell rang. Her heart skipped a beat. She turned towards the door and went to open it. Her heart was beating so loudly in her chest that she was sure that anyone could hear it. She opened the door to see two breathtakingly gorgeous women were standing in front of her. One of them had flaming red hair that went down to her waist. She was taller than Jane with a figure similar to hers. But, Jane was probably the one with the bigger boobs of the two. The other woman had black shoulder-length curls. She was almost the same height as Jane but she had a perky figure.

Jane asked them to come in and they hugged her tightly. The red-haired woman old that her name was Mia, while the woman with the black curls was named Jess. Jess was wearing a short skirt, while Mia was wearing a strapless black dress that just barely covered her ass. They had both brought wine. So, Jane got three glasses from the kitchen and asked them to sit on the couch. When she was about to sit, she saw that Mia's dress was way too short and she could see what was inside. She was wearing nothing. It made her feel like an invisible hand had just pinched her clit.

She poured wine for all of them. She sat on the couch where Jess was sitting so that both of them were sitting across Mia. They casually started talking. She could feel that Jess was inching closer to her rapidly. When

Jane turned around to talk to her she found herself face to face with Jess. Jess held Jane's chin in her hands and pulled her head and kissed her on the lips. Jane had never been kissed by a woman before, and what a shame it was she thought because it was the best kiss she ever had.

Her cheeks were flushed, her breasts were becoming redder too. Moreover, she felt wet. Her pussy was becoming wetter. In no time, Jess had her tongue inside Jane's mouth. Mia walked over and kneeled in front of both of them. She pulled the knot on Jane's robe and t gave away showing her magnificent bosom and body. Mia went on to touch her boobs through the fabric of her clothes. Jane gasped sharply. She had never been touched by a woman before. Mia smiled and deftly removed the lingerie. Now, Jane was completely naked in front of these strangers.

Jess had a hungry look on her face when she saw her huge breasts. "Where were you all my life!" she said and then immediately started sucking on Jane's right tit. Mia followed suit and started licking her left breast. Jane was panting loudly. She even moaned slightly when both of them started licking her nipples. While Mia's mouth was busy on Jane's boob, she slid her hand between Jane's thighs. Jane let out a loud gasp when Mia touched her vagina. "Already wet are you my love?" She said and kneeled down again. She spread Jane's legs far wide, which exposed her pussy to the cool air of the living room. "Oh, God!" She whispered sharply.

Mia rubbed Jane's clit for a while which made Jane groan sensually.  By now, Jess had completely taken charge of both her boobs. Now she was sucking on one while squishing the other one with her hands. Mia spat on Jane's vagina to make it a little moister. Then she pulled her hair back and then went ahead and started licking Jane's pussy. She starting moaning loudly. Jane felt like her entire body was on fire. she furiously pulled Jess by her curls who was sucking on her breasts and pulled her in for a kiss.

They were glued to each other's mouths with their tongues inside each other when Jane had to suddenly stop kissing her. Mia's tongue was sucking and eating her pussy out which was making her come. She was panting sharply. And when she was close, her pants became deeper, and then finally her entire body vibrated, and then she came.

 "Oh my! That is a lot of juices!" Mia said. she pulled Jess down and both of them slurped all of Jane's juices and licked her pussy raw. After that, they kissed each other briefly before coming up for some air. "Let us take this into the bedroom," Jess said. Jane who was lying limp over there after her first massive orgasm could not speak. But she just nodded and got up to go into the bedroom.

By the time they were in the bedroom, Jane had regained her senses, and now she was hungry for more. As soon as they were inside, she pulled Jess's blouse off her body, while Mia, pulled her skirt down. Then both Jane and Jess removed Mia from her dress. Jane realized that none of them were wearing any panties or bras inside.

They went to the bed, but this time Mia had different plans. She made Jane lie down. Then she sat on her face and said, "Lick me! Lick my cunt raw!" Jane obliged. And she started licking Mia's pussy. She had never ever tasted anyone's cunt before, but it wasn't bad she thought.  In fact, it felt amazing to do this. Meanwhile, Jess crouched near Jane's crotch. She started sucking on the nerve bundle. Jane gasped. That is when Mia slapped one of Jane's boobs and said, "Don't stop! Make me come!" And Jane started furiously licking her pussy again. Meanwhile, Jess licked two of her fingers and inserted them inside Jane. Jane's body arched as though asking begging for those fingers to go in deeper.

"You like that don't you!" Jess said while inserting another of her finger. Fr Jane, everything was becoming blur but she kept on licking Mia's pussy who was now screaming, "Yes! Yes! Just like that! Don't stop! Make me come! Make me come on your face!" Mia was rubbing herself on Jane's face while she was licking her. She started heaving. Now, she had closed her eyes and she had pulled one of her boobs closer and she was licking it.

As Mia had said, she came on Jane. All her cum was sprayed on Jane's face. "Eat my cum!" Mia said. and Mia obediently started licking the cum that was still in Mia's pussy. She had never tasted it before but, she liked it. Then, Mia bent down and licked all the cum off Jane's face. Meanwhile, Jess was shoving three of her fingers inside Jane with force. Jane's body was responding to it by trying arching closer and closer.

Now, Jane was about to have her second orgasm. She started panting and moaning. Everything around her had started to seem blurred. She kept saying "Oh my God!" "Please make me come!" She groaned one last time soaking Jess's fingers in her cum. "Here, taste yourself!" Jess said. she put her fingers in Jane's mouth. She licked her fingers. Then, Jess started kissing Jane, and then Mia joined in too.

They could not tell whose tongue was in whom, but one thing was for sure. Everyone had someone else's tongue trying to shove down their throat. It felt like they had been kissing for hours. Finally, Mia got up and went outside in the hall. That is when Jane pushed Jess on the bed. She slowly started sucking her clit. Then she started rubbing her pussy with her hands while sucking on her nerve bundle.

Jess got hold of Jane's hair and started pushing it on her pussy as if to make her entire tongue go inside her vagina. She was writhing and moaning while Jane was making it insanely slow and intense for Jess. She was her up for a huge orgasm. Jane had never been in a situation where she had to do something like this to a woman. But, she went with her instincts and did whatever that felt right and judging by the Jess's moans, she figured that she had got it right.

When Jane was in the middle of the session, Mia had come back with something in her hands. Jane did not recognize it, but is suspiciously looked like cocks with some kind of harness on them. Jane did not know what she was supposed to do with that, but like everything she was doing that day, she figured she will learn it along the way.

Mia had in fact brought something interesting. She had brought strap-ons. Jane looked a little confused. Mia smiled and said, "Don't worry. I will teach you. Here!" she said, and threw one towards her. She caught it deftly and then watched Mia as she was putting it on. It wasn't that hard. She did what she saw. And then Mia motioned her towards Jess. Mia spit on the cock first to lubricate it a little and then she told Jane to insert it inside Jess. "This is what it feels like to be on the other side of the cock." She said.

Jane was excited to try this out. When she first inserted the strapon inside Jess, she thrusted it.  What she was not planning on was that it was going to pleasure her too. With every thrust, the strap on was pleasuring Jane's clit too. Now, the more she played with it the more pleasure both of them got. Both of them were panting and moaning. When she saw that Jane had gotten the hang of it, she went near her Jess's mouth and she started using it as a hole to put it in. and this way, all the three ladies were giving and gaining pleasure from each other. It was Jess who came first, then it was Jane.

Jess sat up and put her hand between Jane's thighs and cupped all the juices in her hands. Jane did the same with Jess's cum and they went and put it all on Mia's face and breasts.

Then they started licking it. They started licking and sucking her tits and her navel. When Jane was sucking on her navel, Jess went up to Mia's throat and bit her gently. Then she started sucking on it. Mia was thrashing and groaning uncontrollably. That is when Jane got up, removed Mia's strapon, and threw it on the bed. Then she inserted it inside Mia and started fucking her. First, she went with a gentle pace, and then she moved it up a notch, and then she went faster and faster. As she was shoving the dildo inside her, she could feel that her clit was being stimulated too.

She was biting on her lower lip trying not to moan, but she was not very successful. She gave in and let out a huge moan. That is when Jess got up, put on the strap-on that Mia was using. Things were about to get wild.

"Let us have some fun." She said. She put her spit on the cock and then she sat on her knees near Jane and then motioned her to stop riding. Then she put her strap-on inside Mia too. She was gasped very loudly. "Do you want me to stop?" Jess asked her. "Please don't stop! Yes, just like that." Said Mia who was in a whole different world. She was nearing her orgasm when she got up, shoved Jess on the bed and sat on the dildo, and started riding it. Both of them were moaning like anything.

Jane removed the strap-on that was on her. Then she went and sat on Jess's face. She immediately started licking her. Now, Jane and Mia were facing each other. Jane could see Mia's boobs going up and down as she was riding her while being licked by Jess. It reminded her of one of the scenes from the book, where the protagonist was in the same situation as her. She felt so kinky thinking about it, and she was gad as hell that her husband had found out about her dirty secret. If he hadn't. she would still have been stuck with the books and her hand to try and be in absolute bliss. But now she didn't have to, she was actually experiencing it.

Soon enough, Mia came. Then she leaned in to kiss Jane like it was the most natural thing to do. Jane felt so too. She also, leaned in so that they could share a kiss. Jane and Mia, who were both sitting on Jess, got up and laid down on her side. All of them were a little exhausted and thirsty. Jane got up and got the wine from the living room. When she entered she saw that Jess and Mia were sitting and kissing each other while both touching each other's pussy.

All of them drank the wine straight from the bottles. They soon got their energy back. Mia pulled Jane and made her lie on the bed. Then she started licking her very wet pussy. Jane was in a state of euphoria. She had never wanted to be with her husband for so long, but when she was with Mia and Jess, she felt like the night should never end.

When Mia was crouched while licking Jane, Jess went towards her back and started fucking her hole from behind. She was slapping her ass and roughly plowing into her. Jane thought it may hurt Mia, but she was wrong. She saw that Mia quite enjoyed it. But, that train of her thought was completely broken when Mia, who was licking her pussy, started sucking on her clit. She could feel her whole body shudder and thrash. And then, she came. She could only see spots in front of her eyes.

Jane had a satisfied smile on her face that was covered in sweat. She thought that the night could not get any better than this. But, she was wrong. She saw that Jess and Mia, both were wearing strapons. It was Jane's turn to be double penetrated. Jane never knew she could feel such strong emotions. She was so satisfied and yet so hungry. The entire night continued in the same fashion, where everyone had everything done to them.

When they finally slept, it was almost three o'clock in the night. Nobody bothered to put on clothes. They just slept there, naked, beside each other without a care in the world. In the morning when they got up, Jane poured some orange juice for everyone and made sandwiches. While having breakfast they were casual, kissing or touching each other. Finally, when it was time to leave, they kissed each other goodbye and exchanged phone numbers. This wasn't the last time she was going to see Jess and Mia.

She thought that this one night was going to satisfy her need, but she was wrong. Instead, it had awakened a sleeping monster. Now, she wanted more and more of it. Just when she was making plans in her mind, she heard the doorbell ring. She went to see who it was. It was Alan. "I thought you were on a business trip," Jane said jokingly while kissing her husband.

"Well, there was another business I had to attend to too." He said, lifting her in his arms. "I see. So how was your business." She asked him when he put her down on the coffee table. "Let us just say that I know a busty blonde who could replace you when you are, umm, how do we put it? Yes, busy elsewhere." He said with a sly smile. "Oooh, did you now! Tell me all about it!" Jane said.

"How about I show you he said," Alan said, pulling her closer to him. "And how would you do that?" Jane asked him in a teasing tone. "Like this." He unbuttoned his pants and put his cock inside her which was still wet from last night's activities. He smiled to himself thinking that finally his wife was happy and kept on pounding inside her.

# STELLA AND JOSH

Stella and Josh were the perfect couples. They had built a perfect life for themselves. They had a big and beautiful house, they were rolling in money, and they were madly in love.

The couple was wild. In fact, they had met each other through very interesting circumstances. They had met each other through a friend's 'pool party' where people were more concerned about getting busy with strangers rather than enjoying the pool. Not that it was completely ignored, the pool. It had a very crucial part to play in all the rendezvous that night.

It was a night to remember for the both of them. Stella was in the pool sipping on a Margherita. She was wearing a red-hot bikini that left little to the imagination. She had curves to die for. She was easily the sexiest girl over there, not that there wasn't any competition.

And Josh, well he was busy too. He was busy hooking up with a petite blond when his eyes fell on a ravishing brunette in the pool wearing a sexy bikini. How he had missed her before is still a mystery for him. And so, he took the leave of the girl who was in his arms. She looked disappointed at first, but then she found another guy standing beside her who was ready to start off where Josh had stopped.

"Hi. I haven't seen you around before," said Josh to the mysterious lady in the pool. "Well, I haven't been around before," she said, with a crooked smile that made him go crazy. "I am Josh, and you are?" he asked her. "Stella," she said while extending her hand for a handshake. He grabbed her hand and pulled her in for a kiss. It was the most intense kiss the both of them ever had.

Maybe it was the one too many Margherita, or maybe it was the pool or the man who was sending sparks through her entire body with the fiercest kiss she ever had, but she was wet. And at that moment, she knew that she had found her match. And that is how their story began.

It had been two years to their marriage, and nothing could have been better. Except, sometimes she felt that maybe she was craving some adventures. I mean, she was very happy with him, but she felt like she wanted something more. Every aspect of the wedding was great, except maybe the monogamy. She decided that it was time she talked to her husband about it.

That day, she came home early. She drew up a bubble bath for herself. She put in some lavender oil in it, Josh loved it. After a forty-five-minute bath, she stepped out of the bathroom, smelling heavenly because of her lavender essence. She went into her closet to figure out what she wanted to wear today.

Well seeing as it was important to keep her husband in high spirits, she decided to wear the black lingerie that, as he perfectly describes, was teasing. It was tight and silky enough to highlight her curves and flimsy enough that it would tear apart easily if wanted. She combed her waist-length hair so that it was shining. Josh was in for an amazing night.

When Josh came home, she called him from the bedroom itself. "Josh! Can you come in?" she said in the sincerest voice. "In a minute honey!" he said. He freshened up in the downstairs bathroom and went up only to see that his lovely, naughty wife was sitting on the bed showing off her juicy body. It was tantalizing for him.

"You are so naughty." He said while unbuttoning his shirt. "let me help you with it" she said. she went over to him and quickly removed his white shirt that was barely hiding his ripped body. She started kissing him hungrily. There was an urgency in the way she was biting his lower lip. She put her hand through his dark brown curls and tugged slightly.

He pushed her on the dressing table and started sucking on her neck. Her whole body felt like it was on fire. She closed her eyes and bit her lip. She was holding her right boob in her hand, while with her left hand she was trying to pull Josh more closer to her. But the dressing table was proving to be a challenge. She unwantingly stopped him and pushed him on the bed. She got on top of him and started kissing his beautiful lips rapidly.

Josh could not take it anymore. He grabbed her and pulled her down, and got on top of her. He put his hand between her legs. It sent shivers down her spine. "Oh babe, you are so wet!" he said. He played with her clit by still keeping the fabric in place. He started rubbing her vagina through her flimsy lingerie. While his one hand was busy pleasuring her pussy, his other hand started playing with her right nipple. She gave out a small moan.

Josh decided that the lingerie had created enough disturbance. He untied the knots of her panties. She let out a gasp. He quickly tried to untie the knots of her upper part of the garment. But, it was way too fiddly, and he was getting impatient. He quickly tore it away, sending another shiver through her entire body. He started sucking on her boobs one by one. While still rubbing her clit.

Stella knew she was close to her first orgasm. Josh also sensed the same and he increased his speed of rubbing. She was biting her lip so hard. Josh decided to turn it up a notch. He went further down and started licking the lips of her pussy. Her breathing started increasing rapidly. Her vagina was responding to his touch with a lot of vigor. She was holding her pillow and trying her best to keep as still as possible. And now she was about to come. Her entire body shivered and then she went limp.

Her juices started oozing out, and Josh slurped all of them. He licked her pussy clean. Once Stella came back to normal, she pushed Josh on the bed and unzipped his pant, and threw it below the bed. His cock was rock hard now. She pinned him down and then put his cock inside her wet pussy. She adjusted it properly and then she began thrusting him inside her. At first, she kept the pace slow. And then gradually she started increasing the pace.

Josh was holding on to her wrists and pushing her hard on his cock. "Fuck me, babe! Come on! Faster! Faster!" He yelled. Stella quickened her pace. It was getting intense. She started moaning with every thrust because every thrust made her feel like she was nearing heaven. She went on and on until she knew both of them were nearing an orgasm.

That is when she slowed down again. He let out a grunt. She was now thrusting him deep and slow.

Both of them came at the same time. Her pussy was filled with all his juices as well as her. When she got off him, she cupped some of the mixtures in her hands and made him lick them. He licked it off and then pulled her in for a kiss. It was a passionate and steamy kiss that seemed to have gone on for ages.

Tired, Stella was lying on Josh's chest. Josh was idly caressing her hair. That is when she decided to prop the question. "You know what I was thinking?" she asked him. "what?" he questioned back. "I think we need an adventure!" with a little hint of excitement. "What did you have in mind?" he asked curiously, knowing full well that his wife was capable of coming up with truly wild escapades. "You know what would be great? If we got to sleep with other people, rather another couple who is just as crazy as us!" she said, now lying on her stomach facing her husband.

"Are you suggesting you want to swing?" Josh asked. "Yes. I mean I don't have a couple in mind yet, but how cool would that be?" She asked him expectantly. "Now that I think about it, it doesn't seem like such a bad idea. We could definitely do this!" Josh said.

"I knew you were the right man for me!" she said ecstatically and kissed him. "Ready for round two?" he asked. "You bet!" she said, cloyingly. He pinned her down to the bed and then pushed his long shaft inside her and they started from where they had left off.

When the next morning arrived, Stella got up first a went downstairs for a cup of black coffee. The conversation had gone better than she had anticipated. It got her thinking that maybe Josh had been thinking about this on his own too.

"Hey," Josh said. He kissed her on the neck from behind. "Good morning, there is coffee in the pot." She said. "So, I was thinking about your idea and I think I may have a couple in mind." He said while pouring himself a cup of hot coffee "This fast? My goodness! Someone seems eager!" she said joking. Josh just smiled and took a sip from his cup. "So, who is it?" She asked. "Now who is impatient?" He said tauntingly. "Oh, come on!" She said she was curious to know who he was thinking about.

"You remember Jill?" He asked her. "Your step-sister?" Stella asked enquiringly. "Yes. She is in town with her fiancé." He said. "Well, what has that got to do with us?" Stella asked impatiently. "Well, she and her beau are also, how do you put it, yes, into polygamy," said Josh. "First of all, no one says that. And second of all, how do you know that?" asked Stella. "That is not important. What is important is, what do you think about them as our swing partners?" asked Josh. "It won't get uncomfortable for you?" Stella asked. "Jill and I have crossed that bridge long ago. And turns out, we like this side of our relationship better," said Josh.

"Ooohh! You have a naughty past! I like it! Well, I have no problem if you have no problem. And what do you know about her fiancé ?" added Stella. "Well, his name is Mike and he owns a gym. You would be quite pleased with him." Josh said with his naughty smile. "I better be," Stella said.

A week went by after their discussion. Stella had gotten busy in her job. It was an exceptionally difficult week. But, Josh had not at all let it slip from his mind. He was going about trying to set it up with Jill. He did not wish to talk about these things over the phone so he wanted to meet her in person and talk about it.

He had called her right after he had left for the office on the day of he had the conversation with Stella. She was going to be busy so they decided to meet two days later. They met in a restaurant and talked things over.

She had no problem, of course, but she said she had to discuss this with her fiancé. She told him that whatever the answer is she will let him know over the phone in a day or two. Josh wasn't sure what was to be expected. But he was hopeful. He had seen his half-sister after a very long time and he had forgotten how hot she was. It had been a while since they had their hands on each other, but after meeting her, the flames had been reignited.

And so she did call. "Hey, Josh! It's me, Jill. So, I talked to Mike. He wants to do it. Is Sunday okay with you?" she asked. John was beside himself. He told her he will ask Stella if Sunday worked for her. He knew she had been wrapped up in work. It was going to come as a pleasant surprise that he had been following up on it.

He reached home from work, and asked her, "So, I was talking to Jill, she said she and Mike are free on Sunday. What about you? Does it work for you?" Stella looked a little clueless at first. But then, she realized a split second later and he could see that she was excited. "Yes it works for me!" she almost screamed excitedly. And so, he just texted her, that they were on for Sunday. He did not know what to expect from it, but he was sure of one thing. It was going to be memorable as hell.

Finally, Sunday arrived. Stella wore a red V-neck top, that went deep, with shorts. Josh wore a simple black t-shirt above his navy blue jeans. They had decided that they were going to meet Jill and her fiancé Mike in their hotel suite.

Stella did not quite remember how Jill looked, after all, she had met her for only a while a long time ago. When they went to their hotel room, Mike opened the door. He was, there was no other word, breathtakingly hot. He was about six feet tall, had a perfectly tanned body with a killer physique. Stella could not wait to get her hands on such a body. It just made her wonder, if the bigger package is so perfect, what about his manhood? It gave her a tingling sensation in her ears and toes to think about it.

When they stepped in, Stella saw Jill for the first time carefully. She had short and silky blonde hair. She had huge almond eyes and big pouty lips. She did not breasts as large as Stella's but, they were still stunning. She was probably two inches shorter than Stella who was about 5'5". "Nice, this was definitely going to work out." She thought to herself.

Jill gave a huge smile when she saw them. She gave Josh a peck on the lips and then she went on to hug Stella. And, Stella did not fail to notice that her hand slid down to her ass and had lingered there for a moment too long. Stella had a wild youth, but she had never been with a woman before. She thought could that day be today?

Josh quickly introduced everyone and then they opened up a wine bottle. All of them sat on the bed very casually. They decided to play strip poker. The rules were very simple, you lose, you remove a part of your clothing, and to make it even more interesting they decided that the person who won the game could ask any of the other participants to take off a part of their clothes.

Jill called room service for a pack of cards and two more bottles of wine as they had already gone through their first two bottles already. Finally, they started playing. Stella was the first one to lose. She did not know whether to be sad that she lost or be excited about the fact that she was going to be strip in front of her sister-in-law and her husband. Stella decided that she would remove her top exposing her black bra, which did not cover much. She thought she would be embarrassed, but when she glanced sideways at Mike who was sitting next to her, she saw that he was hungrily looking at her bosom, it made her feel slightly titillated.

Josh gave her a quick peck on each of her boobs, which did not help her from stopping getting wet. Now, as per their rule, the person who won had to name one person who would have to take off a piece of clothing. "I think, I want to vote Stella," Mike said slyly. Stella had not been expecting this. Now she had to remove her shorts. Everyone was now staring at her semi-naked. Josh and Mike who was sitting on either side just bent over slightly to see her ass which was barely covered by her lacy panties. "How about we focus on the game guys," Jill said, naughtily.

Stella had noticed that she too had been looking at her body the way Mike was looking. It was strangely arousing for her. Next time, Mike lost and Josh won. "Come on babe, it is time for you to show those abs you got," Jill said teasingly. Mike took off his brown shirt to show his perfect abs. Jill gave him a quick kiss and he caught Stella staring at his abs. "You like what you are seeing there?" he asked her. "Very much so." She said lustfully.

Mike sensed it too. He bent over and kissed her on the mouth. It wasn't soft, it was passionate but short. He squeezed both her nipples once and went back to his place. It had flushed her boobs and cheeks. Now they were a deep crimson in color. Since Josh had won, he had the power to make someone undress. Stella thought that he was going to say Jill, but she saw that Jill motioned in her direction. Josh understood what she meant. "I vote…Stella." He said. "Hey that is cheating!" she said. "Everything is fair in sex sweety," Jill said. Before she could retaliate, Josh unhooked her bra from the back. Stella felt a gasp escaping her. Jill quickly moved ahead and pulled it off her body. Now, Stella's breasts were on show for everybody to look at. "My My My! What do we have here!" Jill said. She moved ahead and went on to cup her large boobs in both her hands, something she had been dying to do ever since Stella had lost the first round and had to remove her top.

Stella had not been touched by a woman like this ever before and it was so invigorating. Her nipples were starting to perk up. Jill moved in and gave her a wet kiss on her mouth. Stella had thought that kissing a woman was going to be so awkward but turns out that it was actually the best experience because they knew what was exactly wanted.

Jill nibbled on Stella's lower lip, it was one of her 'spots.' And in the meanwhile, she was smooshing her boobs with both her hands.

They had gotten into a rhythm of kissing. When they stopped to catch some air, Stella removed Jill's top and she was unhooking her bra when Mike swooped in from behind and licked her neck. Then he put his hands around her and started pinching her nipples. She let out a gasp. As their naked bodies touched each other, she could feel her body heating up.

Meanwhile, Josh took up the job that Stella had left incomplete. He completely removed her bra, and removed her short skirt too, which had been giving him sneak peeks of her butt. He started sucking and licking her breasts. Stella was breathing rapidly now. "It has been a long time since you have had my boobs in your mouth, dear brother." She said, holding his curls and pulling him in so that he could cover a larger surface area. He heard it and then bit one of her boobs. "Aahh!" she gasped. It did not hurt her, but it was definitely making her loins ache. "Oh, I have missed you." She said, keeping closing her eyes and smiling in pleasure.

Meanwhile, Stella had turned around to be face to face with Mike. He began licking her boobs and neck. Occasionally sucking here and there at random so that she was not expecting it. Stella was liking it. Josh had never done this before, it was extremely arousing. It felt to her as though her whole body wanted nothing but Mike's tongue everywhere. As though he had understood what she had said, he pushed her on the bed and pulled her closer to him. She giggled in excitement.

Mike took his wine glass which was on the bedside table. Three-quarters of the wine was gone. But how much ever was left was enough for what he had in mind for her. He poured it in her naval. It started trickling down her sides. So, he furiously started licking all the wine that her naval could not hold. When he was clearing away the last trickle, he made it insanely slow. Stella wasn't sure if her body could handle so much stimulation and not come. Her hips started rising. Her body wanted Mike to lick her naval raw. He started licking with increased vigor he held her hips with both hands to get better support. Stella's breathing had become ragged. She was gasping at every lick now. She could feel that each lick was making her come close to an orgasm. All she could think about now was having his cock inside her taking her above and beyond her pleasure limits.

On the other hand, the stepbrother and sister seemed more at ease with each other than the other couple. Jill had taken off Josh's clothes and now she was giving him a blowjob. Josh wanted to hold her hair in his hands and direct her to put more force and go deeper, but her short hair did not come into his hands. So he just kept ramming her head on his cock vigorously so that she was taking his entire cock in, which was an achievement in itself as he was more endowed than the average man.

She gagged and came up for air. That is when she started playing with his balls. She playfully licked them while caressing his cock with her hand. Josh was grunting. He never made much noise during these amorous activities, but it was by far the best blowjob he ever had. Jill increased her speed and was now putting the cock in and out of her mouth with so much ferocity that Josh was ready to come any minute now. She could sense it too, as his grunts were getting higher and his body was also trying its best to shove his cock in her mouth.

Here, Stella was so ready to have Mike inside her now, that her body was constantly arching towards him. He finally took off his pants. His cock was fully erect. Her eyes widened looking at it. Her pussy was aching for it to be inside her. He adjusted her hips properly so that he had the best angle. And then he took hold of both her legs and then he spread them as wide as he could. She let out a loud gasp. She was not at all expecting this, but nevertheless, she was loving it. He took one of her thighs and bit her there. It was one of her most sensitive erogenous spots. She moaned loudly. "That is right baby! Moan harder." And saying so, he started sucking on the place where he had bitten her.

She was so aroused right now. Everything became blurry as she had closed her eyes so tight in reflex. All she could see were black spots in front of her eyes. She had never been stimulated so much in her entire life. As he was sucking on her juicy thighs, she started shuddering violently, and then with the last shiver, she had her first organism of the day. "Oh look at your pussy! Got any juices for me?" he asked naughtily. And he put his hands near her lips and collected all the fluids he could and he smeared it all over her boobs and face. And then he called out to Jill.

"Hey Jill, look what I have for you to lick," Mike called out. She went over hungrily and started licking all over her boobs. Seeing another man playing with his wife's vagina, and seeing his step-sister licking her boobs and face was making him so erect. He simply had to shove it in someone's hole now. And that is when he saw his opportunity. Jill was crouched on her knees and her elbows like a hungry cat. He went on from the back, interrupted her licking for a moment. He jammed his two fingers in her mouth and wet them with her spit. She was giving him the most vulgar look right now.

He himself spit on his fingers again and wet Jill's pussy, not that it needed any. It was already so moist, that it was almost dripping. He got a hold of her perfectly round ass, inserted his huge hard dick in her pussy. She gave out a little moan. She looked over at him and went backward to give him an urgent kiss. And then she went on to licking Stella's face. He started thrusting inside her. They were long hard thrusts. Each time his balls made contact with her body there was a huge slapping sound. Jill was feeling it. His every thrust was making her body shake, thrash, and just lose control completely.

Meanwhile, seeing as he had cleared away the last remnants of her previous orgasm, he decided that it was time he gave her body what it was begging for so long, his long and erect penis.

He pulled her closer and put her legs around his necks. And then he started pushing inside her. Her body had been anticipating this for so long that the first-ever thrust made her moan loudly. She feared that her eyes would roll back in her brain because every time he thrust inside her, she just rolled back in pleasure.

Near here, her husband was fucking his stepsister who was moaning loudly too.

The fact that her husband was having sex with his stepsister on the same bed as she was having her pussy fucked by that step sister's fiancé made the entire situation even kinkier for her. Slowly both of them were moaning together in a rhythm. There was no competition between the ladies but every moan was louder than the previous one. The two ladies locked eyes and they could see that each of their eyes was filled with nothing but pleasure.

Jill was the first one to come out of the four as it was her first orgasm of the day. Now Stella decided that it was time she took part in some action. She went over towards Jill. She made her husband remove his cock from Jill's pussy and she bent and began licking Jill's clit. She had never done this before, so she wasn't sure if she was doing it right, but a low guttural moan from Jill told her that she was doing the right thing.

She used up all the juices that had come out of her by rubbing and licking it off from her clit. Jill was thrashing around by now. Stella put her fingers in Jill's mouth and she moistened them up. She took one of the fingers and put it in her hole. She then realized that there was room for more fingers, and so she put three more of her fingers, the last one took some effort so that now there were four fingers in Jill's vagina.

Jill let out a large gasp. "Yes! Yes! Yes! Just like that! Keep going! Don't stop!" she kept saying. She was cupping her own boobs and pinching her nipples just to do something so that she wouldn't lose her mind. Stella was fingering her hard and she could feel that her pussy was getting very very wet. The boys were observing this highly arousing scenario and decided that it was time to jump in again.

Josh took up his previous position of fucking someone doggy style. It did not matter to him at the moment whose hole he was going to penetrate as long as he had one. He started ramming himself into his wife while she was fingering his step-sister. Mike went near Jill's breasts and started nibbling and sucking on them. He would occasionally pinch Stella's nipples too which were moving back and forth as Josh was pushing his shaft inside her. Finally, Jill shuddered and had a very huge orgasm. She lay limp while Stella took her finger which was soaking from the fluids from Jill's pussy and put two of them in Mike's mouth and then kissed him while putting her tongue inside him. He followed suit and caught up with it.

Meanwhile, she was holding out her remaining two fingers for Josh. She wanted him to have a taste of her too. She motioned towards him while still glued to Mike's mouth. Josh came and put her fingers in his mouth and licked all of the juices. Stella unglued herself from Mike and started kissing her husband, passionately. Meanwhile, Jill had somewhat come back from her state of euphoria to normal. So Mike bent down and started kissing her.

They had some more wine. And now it was time for round two. Things were about to get heated up even more. Stella was lying on the bed and Jill got on top of her. Now, both of them were facing each other's vaginas. They slowly started teasing around with the clit. Then slowly they started licking the lips of their vagina. Both of them were so into it that they had forgotten that there were men around, but not for long.

Josh and Mike felt that the holes had been empty for quite a while now and they thought each hole deserved a cock. So, Josh decided to fuck his wife's hole, while Mike started fucking his fiancé. All four of them were panting moaning and thrashing around. It was a miracle that the bed had not broken by now because of how intense their activities were getting. They were sure that all the passers-by were going to get a kick out of hearing them. There were sounds of women moaning and calling names, and there noises of panting and grunting that the people in the neighboring room could hear. It was evident to them that we're more than just one man and woman in the room adjacent to them.

Inside the room, four of them were at the peaks of their orgasms. They were a little more intense than their previous ones. The women were exhausted, physically not sexually. Sexually they could still go on for a very long time. But, the boys were not so tired yet. Working out in the gym had finally worked out for them.

Now they decided that it was time to change partners again. Josh took Jill, while Mike went ahead and to have it with Stella. Both of the girls were just lying on the bed waiting for the boys to just take them. Stella was glad to see that the boys had decided it was time for them to change partners. It is not that she did not like Josh or something. But, how many times did she ever get to have her hole by someone other than her husband?

The girls were lying side by side on the beds while the boys got up on them and started fucking them like there was no tomorrow. Mike was pushing in so hard that Stella feared she was going to hurt her head on the panel of the bed. She held the pillow that was under her head to get in some support. So that she did not crash into the wall.

Soon the girls started moaning. Their pussies had become so sensitive that any minor stimulation was enough to put them in a state of complete pleasure. The bed was shaking so violently, that Josh decided to move over to the couch. He picked up Jill, his cock still in her pussy, he was kissing her roughly on the lips and when they reached the couch, he threw her on it. He made her sleep on the couch and then he pulled her legs up so that her hips were just barely on the couch. He caught both her legs and started thrusting inside her. He wasn't getting a good angle so he got a pillow from the bed and put it under her hips. And, then he started fucking her hole again, but it was very hard. Jill barely had time to catch a breath.

Meanwhile, Stella was just taking the hard cock inside her very eagerly. Mike reduced his pace and started grinding on her very slowly.  She was thrashing madly underneath him. He again increased his speed and started pounding her, and then again reduced it. He was playing with her like this until she shuddered violently letting out a loud moan. Her entire body went completely limp. She thought she would never be able to walk again. She looked over to see that her husband was very busy shoving himself inside his step-sister. Her moans were getting louder and louder while his shoves started getting harder. She knew both of them were close to an orgasm. His loudest grunt told her that her husband had come inside her and she had reached hers too.

Jill limped across to the bed and lay down near Stella. Mike and Josh sat on the couch sipping wine. Jill was just casually caressing Stella's pussy. But, Stella moaned slightly. So, that is when Jill quickened her pace. Stella did not understand why this was affecting her so much. And she started biting her lip. That is when Jill got an idea.

She got up and sat on Stella's left leg and then she took her right leg in her hand and she slowly started grinding on her pussy. The lips of their pussy were touching. It was sending sparks down both their bodies. As Jill got the hang of it, she started gaining speed. Soon she was tribbing hard with Stella. They had a rhythm going. They were looking into each other's eyes and making it more intense and passionate.

The boys were enjoying the scene. Josh went with half a glass of wine and poured it on their pussies that were smushing together in the most erotic way possible. He then went on to sit on the couch and watch them doing it. When both of them were nearing their orgasm, their pants became more ragged. First, Jill started shuddering violently and then came. But, she knew that Stella wasn't quite there and so she kept on tribbing till Stella too gave in and came.

Stella pinned Jill on the bed and kissed her on the mouth. Her last orgasm had left her wanting more. She got on top of her and took the same position that she was in, and then she started grinding on her pussy. Jill was not prepared for a second round. But, her hungry vagina was craving for it. Stella was much stronger than Jill. So when she started grinding herself on Jill, Jill was in bliss. She never wanted her to stop at all. And then Stella wanted to make sure that this time, they both came together. She went on and on until both of them felt that they were about to cum. It was the last orgasm that they could handle.

The bed was big enough for the four of them.
So, they slept on it together, a little cramped
but still alright. Josh was sleeping with his
hand on Stella, while she was sleeping beside
Jill who was spooning with her fiancé.

The next day Josh and Stella had taken a leave
from their work as they were too tired to
work. They hugged and kissed Jill and Mike.
It was an experience they were never going to
forget. And Stella was sure that they were
going to miss office a lot more times on
Monday as this was not the last time they
were going to swing with them.